Team PJ Masks

Based on the episode
"Soccer Ninjalinos"

Ready-to-Read

Simon Spotlight
New York London Toronto Sydney New Delhi

This book is based on the TV series PJ MASKS © Frog Box / Entertainment One UK Limited / Walt Disney EMEA Productions Limited 2014;
Les Pyjamasques by Romuald © (2007) Gallimard Jeunesse. All Rights Reserved.
This book/publication © Entertainment One UK Limited 2019.

SIMON SPOTLIGHT
An imprint of Simon & Schuster Children's Publishing Division
1230 Avenue of the Americas, New York, New York 10020
This Simon Spotlight edition December 2019
Adapted by May Nakamura from the series PJ Masks
All rights reserved, including the right of reproduction in whole or in part in any form.
SIMON SPOTLIGHT, READY-TO-READ, and colophon are registered trademarks of Simon & Schuster, Inc.
For information about special discounts for bulk purchases, please contact Simon & Schuster Special Sales at 1-866-506-1949 or business@simonandschuster.com.
Manufactured in the United States of America 1119 LAK
10 9 8 7 6 5 4 3 2 1
ISBN 978-1-5344-5340-1 (hc)
ISBN 978-1-5344-5339-5 (pbk)
ISBN 978-1-5344-5346-3 (eBook)

Amaya, Connor, and Greg
are playing soccer.

Amaya scores a goal.

"You are one star player!"

Greg says.

Then Connor sees
a large Sticky Splat.
This is a job
for the PJ Masks!

Amaya becomes Owlette!

Greg becomes
Gekko!

Connor becomes
Catboy!

They are the PJ Masks!

The PJ Masks find the Ninjalinos.

They are playing

Sticky Splat soccer.

The Sticky Splat hits a car and puffs up like a balloon!

"We are going to splat the whole city!"
Night Ninja says.

Team PJ Masks

springs into action.

"Meet Owlette,
our star player!"
Gekko says.

Owlette races toward the
Sticky Splat ball.

Owlette is about to kick the ball away when she gets splatted!

The Ninjalinos kick
the ball into the school!

Owlette tells her teammates
not to worry.

She still wants to be
the star player.

The soccer game
begins again.

The Ninjalinos
are too powerful!

Owlette wants to give up.
She does not feel like
a star player.

Then Catboy and Gekko
have an idea.

Owlette can fly in the sky
and coach them to victory!

She will be a star player

in a whole new way!

"Time to splat
your Headquarters!"
Night Ninja says.

"Catboy! Use your Super Cat Speed to block the Ninjalinos!" Owlette says.

Night Ninja steals the ball and kicks it toward Headquarters!

"Bend it like Gekko!"

Owlette shouts.

Gekko kicks the ball away!

"Game over!"
Owlette says as the
PJ Masks defeat Night Ninja.

The PJ Masks

can do anything

when they work as a team!

PJ Masks all shout hooray!

Because in the night,

we saved the day!